# WE ARE ALL IN THE DUMPS

WITH

# JACK AND GUY

HELP?
OPEN ON THIS SIDE ONLY
TWO NURSERY RHYMES WITH PICTURES

WE ARE ALL IN THE DUMPS
WITH JACK
AND GUY
BY
MAURICE
SENDAK
JACK
GUY

LYNN!
ARE!
Michael di Capua Books
HarperCollins Publishers
PRIVATE PROPERTY

FOR MARC LINA
HELP?
BEAT IT!
JACK
GUY
FROM
ALLEN
TO
DR. DAVID

JACK
GUY
LOOK WHAT THEY DID!
LOOK WHAT THEY DID!
THE RATS
STOLE THE KITTENS
FROZEN FOODS

WE ARE ALL IN THE DUMPS
AND THE POOR LITTLE KID!
UNEEDA BISCUIT
HELP

RASCAL!
THIEF!

LET'S PLAY BRIDGE
LET'S PLAY FOR THE KITTENS AND THE POOR LITTLE KID!

FOR DIAMONDS ARE TRUMPS

HELP?

LOST!
TRICKED
TRUMPED
DUMPED!
TOWER

THE KITTENS ARE GONE TO ST. PAUL'S!

ST. PAUL'S BAKERY
AND ORPHANAGE

METRO REPORT
DISTINCTIVE HOMES
COME & SEE!
REAL ESTATE
VERY SMART LIVING
FROM 79,0
NO KIDS ALLOWE
PROFIT FROM OUR LOSSES
INVEST IN PROPERT
BUY! BUY!
SHORT TERM
MORTGAGE MONEY AVAILABLE 50,00000 TO 500 000 00!!!!
YARD SALE!
FINE HOMES
HOW YOU CAN AFFOR
OWN HOUSE
50,000 0000
1 YEAR ADJUSTABLE
VERY SMART LIVING!
7%
WANT A KITTY TO CUDDLE?

HELP?
ST. PAUL'S BAKER
AND ORPHANAGE

# THE BABY IS BIT

# THE MOON'S IN A FIT

BABIES
THE NEW YORK TIMES
FAMINE IN THE WORLD
OCT. 17, 1992
JIM GOES HOME

AND THE HOUSES ARE BUILT

# WITHOUT WALLS

# JACK AND GUY

WENT OUT IN THE RYE

ST. PAUL'S BAKERY

ST. PAUL'S BAKERY & ORPHANAGE

# AND THEY FOUND A LITTLE BOY

THE POOR LITTLE KID!
ST. PAUL'S BAKERY & ORPHANAGE

WITH ONE BLACK EYE

BAKERY + ORPHANAGE

COME SAYS JACK LET'S KNOCK HIM

ON THE HEAD

HELP
JACK

# NO SAYS GUY

# LET'S BUY HIM SOME BREAD

OH
MY

# YOU BUY ONE LOAF

AND I'LL BUY TWO

AND WE'LL BRING HIM UP

GU

# AS OTHER FOLK DO